THE INVENTOR:
BENJAMIN
FRANKLIN

Melissa A. Settle, M.Ed.

TIPS FOR REHEARSING READER'S THEATER

BY AARON SHEPARD

- Make sure your script doesn't hide your face. If there is anyone in the audience you can't see, your script is too high.

- While you speak, try to look up often. Don't just look at your script. When you do look at the script, move just your eyes and keep your head up.

- Talk slowly. Speak each syllable clearly.

- Talk loudly! You have to be heard by every person in the room.

- Talk with feeling. Your voice has to tell the story.

- Stand or sit up straight. Keep your hands and feet still if they're doing nothing useful.

- If you're moving around, face the audience as much as you can. When rehearsing, always think about where the audience will be.

- Characters, remember to be your character even when you're not speaking.

- Narrators, make sure you give the characters enough time for their actions.

TIPS FOR PERFORMING READER'S THEATER

BY AARON SHEPARD

- If the audience laughs, stop speaking until they can hear you again.

- If someone talks in the audience, don't pay attention.

- If someone walks into the room, don't look at them.

- If you make a mistake, pretend it was right.

- If you drop something, try to leave it where it is until the audience is looking somewhere else.

- If a reader forgets to read his or her part, see if you can read the part instead, make something up, or just skip over it. Don't whisper to the reader!

- If a reader falls down during the performance, pretend it didn't happen.

THE INVENTOR: BENJAMIN FRANKLIN

Characters

Narrator 1

Narrator 2

Deborah

Mr. Franklin

Townsperson

Benjamin

Setting

This reader's theater takes place during the 1770s in America and London.

Benjamin

Deborah

Act 1

Narrator 1: Benjamin Franklin lived many years ago. Even though he became very well known, his life did not start out that way.

Narrator 2: Benjamin was the youngest son in a large family from Boston, Massachusetts.

Deborah: His father was a candle and soap maker.

Mr. Franklin: All of my boys were expected to be tradesmen like me.

Townsperson: But Ben was special. Even though he was only a young boy, we could all tell that he was smart.

Mr. Franklin: I wasn't sure what to do with Ben. I decided to send him to school to learn Latin. Maybe he would grow up to be a preacher.

Benjamin: At first, I didn't know if I would like moving away from my family to go to school. But, I loved it!

Deborah: Ben did really well in school. He was at the top of his class.

Mr. Franklin: After Ben finished his first year of school, I realized that sending him away to school was too expensive.

Townsperson: Mr. Franklin decided to send Ben to a local school where he would learn basic reading, writing, and math skills.

Narrator 2: Benjamin went to that school for two years.

Narrator 1: At the end of two years, Benjamin's father said that he'd had enough school. When Benjamin turned ten, he began to work for his father.

Benjamin: For the next two years, I worked and learned about many different trades. When I turned 12, my father made me pick one trade to master.

Townsperson: Ben had to become an apprentice to someone until he turned 21. That would be nine years!

Benjamin: I liked learning about many different jobs. Nine years learning about one thing was going to be *much* too boring.

Mr. Franklin: Ben was getting older. He needed to figure out what he was going to do with his life. I thought that becoming an apprentice would help him settle down.

Benjamin: Running errands for my dad had helped me see how many wonderful things there were to learn about. I wanted to become a sailor and travel around the world.

Deborah: Ben was afraid to tell his father that he didn't want to become an apprentice.

Narrator 1: Finally, Benjamin gave in to his father's wishes and decided to become an apprentice for his brother James.

Narrator 2: James was a printer in Boston. A printer is someone who writes and publishes things for people to read.

Townsperson: Ben helped his brother set the type on the large printing press. He had to work very hard.

Mr. Franklin: I was happy that Ben decided to go to work for his brother. James would teach Ben many valuable lessons.

Act 2

Benjamin: I loved learning all about being a printer. But, my brother James was too strict with me!

Deborah: Ben didn't think that he would be able to stay in that job for nine long years. He wanted to see the world and learn new things.

Narrator 1: Benjamin worked for James for five years. He learned the printing trade, but that just wasn't enough.

Narrator 2: During those five years, Benjamin spent every free moment reading and learning new things.

Mr. Franklin: Ben started to write poetry. I didn't mind telling him that his poems were horrible.

Townsperson: That didn't stop Ben. He just kept on writing more poems until he got better at it. He always wanted to learn new words.

Mr. Franklin: I must admit that his poems and stories got better with practice.

Townsperson: Ben wasn't just learning new words; he was trying to learn *everything*! That boy's mind never stopped spinning.

Deborah: Once, he read a book on how to swim better. Then, he swam around doing crazy tricks.

Townsperson: He even read a book on how to be nice to others. Ben liked to read more than anyone I've ever met.

Benjamin: Reading gave me answers to the questions that were always swirling around in my head. I wanted to know how *everything* worked.

Townsperson: Ben even read a book on how to argue better.

Benjamin: It seemed to me that I might need to have strong debating skills someday.

Narrator 1: Benjamin spent so much time trying to figure out the world around him, that he never really fit in with his peers.

Poem: Fitting In

Act 3

Narrator 1: When Benjamin was 17, he decided that he didn't want to be an apprentice any more.

Narrator 2: Benjamin decided to run away from his brother's printing shop. In fact, he ran all the way to Philadelphia, Pennsylvania.

Benjamin: It took me a few years, but by 1728, I owned my very own print shop.

Mr. Franklin: Ben was so excited to be making money! He bought new clothes, new shoes, and a fancy watch.

Benjamin: I couldn't wait to show everyone back home how well I was doing.

Townsperson: When Ben had saved some money, he went back to visit his family. James wasn't very happy to see his youngest brother.

Mr. Franklin: James was mad that Ben came back to show off in front of everyone. James and Benjamin didn't talk for two whole years after that!

Act 4

Narrator 2:   Back in Philadelphia, Benjamin was very happy. He had lots of friends that were just like him.

Mr. Franklin: In 1723, Ben met a young woman named Deborah Read. They decided to get married in 1730.

Benjamin: I was 24 years old and I loved being married. Deborah and I worked very well together. We owned a print shop, a bookstore, and a general store.

Townsperson: In their general store, they sold many useful items, including Mr. Franklin's candles and soaps.

Deborah: Ben was always studying strange and interesting things. He even studied how little black ants communicated with one another.

Mr. Franklin: Ben started inventing things to make life easier for people.

Narrator 2: He invented new ways to light city streets at night.

Narrator 1: He also invented bifocals, which are special eyeglasses.

Deborah: Ben invented a wood-burning stove to help heat our house.

Townsperson: He was always creating and inventing new ways to improve people's lives.

Mr. Franklin: He helped form the first fire department and public library in Philadelphia. He even created an insurance company to help people who lost their property in fires.

**Song:
Curious Ben**

Narrator 1: During the early years of his marriage, Benjamin starting publishing an almanac. An almanac is a book that is full of odd and interesting facts.

Benjamin: My almanac, *Poor Richard's Almanack*, was published once a year.

Deborah: Ben's almanac was special because he wrote such clever jokes and advice. The almanac also included weather information, dates of holidays, and even when the moon would be full.

Townsperson: People loved his almanac. He wrote one every year for over 20 years.

Narrator 2: One of Benjamin's most famous lines from his almanac is, "A penny saved is a penny earned." People still repeat that line today!

Townsperson: You might think that "Ben the Inventor" settled down as he got older.

Narrator 1: You'd be wrong. Benjamin still had some of his best ideas to come.

Townsperson: Ben wanted to keep learning new things. He even changed the way mail was sent.

Mr. Franklin: It seemed like Ben could do anything he wanted to do.

Act 5

Narrator 1: Benjamin is very well known today because of his work with electricity.

Narrator 2: Benjamin wasn't the first person to study electricity. He may have just been the first person to put electricity to good use.

Benjamin: Actually, I *didn't* put it to good use at first.

Deborah: Ben used electricity to play tricks on his family and friends.

Benjamin: It was only after time passed that I began to really think hard about how to use electricity. I started to think that maybe lightning and electricity might be made of the same energy.

Deborah: Electricity is no laughing matter. More than once, Ben shocked himself. Some people thought that Ben was crazy. But, I knew better.

Mr. Franklin: One time, Ben wanted to get closer to the lightning in the sky.

Townsperson: There weren't any tall buildings around, so Ben attached a key to a kite string and flew the kite as high as he could.

Deborah: He said that he wanted to see if the lightning would hit the kite and move the shock to his end of the string.

Benjamin: That's right, and guess what? It worked! I felt the shock on my end. I was so excited!

Mr. Franklin: That meant that the electric shock of lightning could travel through a string. He couldn't wait to tell people the exciting news!

Narrator 1: Ben even had friends in Europe that wanted to hear about his experiments with electricity.

Narrator 2:	What Benjamin didn't expect was that his news would travel so fast.
Mr. Franklin:	He was becoming a very famous man!
Deborah:	People started writing him letters and shaking his hand when he walked down the street.
Benjamin:	I'll admit that I was starting to feel very proud of myself.
Deborah:	Ben still wasn't finished, though. He wouldn't be happy until he used lightning to make people's lives easier.
Benjamin:	I placed a special rod on the top of my barn to attract lightning. I called it a lightning rod.
Narrator 1:	Lightning rods helped protect homes and other buildings. Lightning bolts were attracted to the metal rods instead of the roofs of the buildings.
Narrator 2:	So, the lightning bolts didn't catch the buildings on fire. This was how Benjamin helped protect others with his electricity experiments.

Act 6

Narrator 1: During the mid-1700s, the colonists were having a lot of problems with the British leaders. The colonies were under British rule, but the Americans were getting tired of being told what to do all the time.

Narrator 2: In 1757, people in Pennsylvania asked Benjamin to travel to London and talk to the British king and Parliament.

Deborah: They wanted my husband to travel all the way across the ocean to talk to people in London! I knew I would miss him, but I was also very proud of him.

Benjamin: I loved London! I enjoyed buying fancy clothes and jewelry.

Townsperson: Ben bought everything he could get his hands on, from eyeglasses to dishes.

Deborah: Benjamin was such a dear. He was always sending me gifts from London.

Benjamin: I wrote often to Deborah and my children. I had many friends in London, but I missed my family.

Deborah: It was very hard to have Ben gone. But since I was afraid of traveling across the ocean, I couldn't go to London to be with him. His letters were very important to me.

Narrator 1: Benjamin was in London during a time when the king and Parliament were forcing the colonists to pay special taxes.

Mr. Franklin: The Americans had taxes that the people in other parts of Great Britain didn't have. It wasn't fair.

Narrator 2: Benjamin spent almost 20 years in London trying to fight for the rights of the colonists.

Narrator 1: When he finally decided to come home, Benjamin was too late to be with his wife Deborah. She died in 1774 before he returned to Philadelphia.

Act 7

Benjamin: When I returned to Philadelphia in 1775, I was already 69 years old.

Narrator 2: Some people thought that Benjamin might finally be ready to settle down.

Townsperson: How could Ben settle down? He had come back to America to help solve some pretty serious problems.

Narrator 1: In 1775, a war started between America and Great Britain.

Narrator 2: Benjamin wanted to fight in the battles himself.

Narrator 1: The people of the American colonies had a more important job for Benjamin.

Narrator 2: They wanted him to debate some more!

Benjamin: While George Washington commanded the soldiers during the war, I agreed to go to France.

Mr. Franklin: The Americans needed some help to win the war. The colonial leaders decided that Ben should travel to France and ask the king to give his country's full support to our side of the war.

Act 8

Narrator 2: The ocean trip was hard for Benjamin. He got very sick on the way across.

Narrator 1: When Benjamin got to France he was so sick that he couldn't get dressed up to meet people.

Deborah: His hair was crazy and he wore a fur hat. There weren't even any wigs that he could find to cover his hair.

Townsperson: None of the wigs would fit him right!

Narrator 1: The people of France just loved Benjamin! They considered him a hero in his plain clothes and funny hat.

Narrator 2: Benjamin got to right work even though he was so sick. He worked very hard to get France to join America in the war.

Benjamin: It finally worked, and France agreed to help the colonists fight the American Revolution.

Act 9

Townsperson: When Ben returned home to America, people couldn't wait to see their hero.

Narrator 1: He was now 79 years old.

Townsperson: Most of us thought that he would live a quieter life now. But again, we were wrong. Ben had important things to do still!

Benjamin: I helped some great men write the Constitution of the United States. I was very honored to be part of that group.

Narrator 2: During this key time in the new country's history, Benjamin thought back to a book he had read so long ago.

Benjamin: It was a book that taught me how to argue better and treat people right.

Narrator 1: It's funny how he knew that reading and learning would help him so much in his life.

Mr. Franklin: It certainly did. He is one of the most important and honored inventors and statesmen of the 1700s.

FITTING IN

When people say your ideas are wrong,
You may feel as though you don't belong.

They might oppose the way you think,
And your confidence may start to shrink.

But stay strong! To yourself be true.
Remember no other is quite like you.

So, when you feel you don't fit in,
Know that you fit in *your own* skin.

You are you, the only one.
Just be yourself, and your race is won!

 CURIOUS BEN

Who invented the lightning rod?
Ben Franklin, that's who!
Who invented batteries?
Ben Franklin did that too!

Curious Ben, Curious Ben,
Science was the key
That helped you on your way
With each discovery.

Who invented the fire department?
Ben Franklin, that's who!
And the lending library?
Ben Franklin did that too!

Curious Ben, Curious Ben
You're an inspiration
Always full of bright ideas
That helped to build our nation.

Who invented the lightning rod?
Ben Franklin, that's who!
If we find a bright idea,
We can be inventors too!

GLOSSARY

almanac—(OL-muh-nak) a book printed once a year that contains information of general interest

apprentice—(uh-PREN-tis) a person who is learning a trade or art by working under a skilled worker

bifocals—(BYE-fo-kuhlz) glasses with two parts, one corrects for distance vision and one corrects for near vision

Constitution of the United States—document that outlines the laws that govern the United States

debating—discussing a question by presenting arguments

Parliament—(PAR-luh-muhnt) the British legislative branch that represents its people and makes its laws

printing press—a machine that produces multiple copies of a document

shock—a strong charge of electricity passing through the body of a person

statesmen—a person who works in the government of a country

taxes—money paid to the government for services or to be able to use something

trades—occupations requiring manual or mechanical skill

tradesmen—workers in a skilled trade